SO-CCK-025

ST. JEROME'S SCHOOL LIBRARY
El Cerrito, California

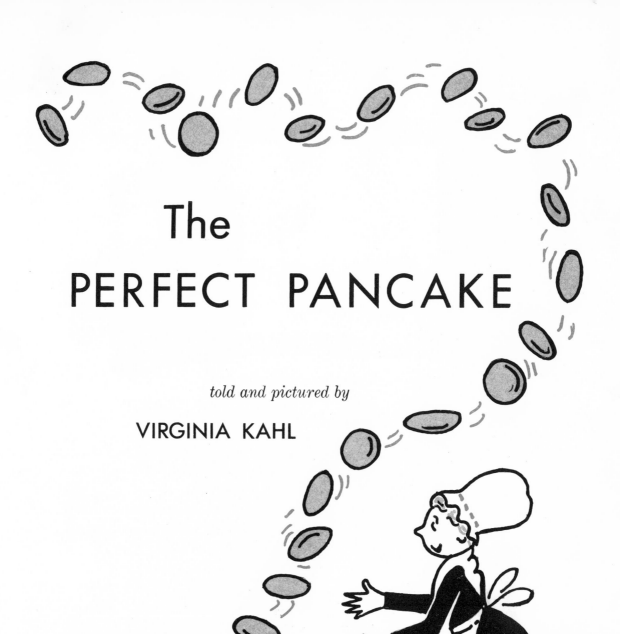

The
PERFECT PANCAKE

told and pictured by

VIRGINIA KAHL

CHARLES SCRIBNER'S SONS   New York

Copyright © 1960 VIRGINIA KAHL   *All rights reserved.*   Printed in the United States of America   G-1.73 [RLD]

SBN 684-92305-X [RB]

ST. JEROME'S SCHOOL LIBRARY
El Cerrito, California

There once was a lady, the one in this book,
Who was known as a perfectly marvelous cook.
Whenever she happened to stir up and bake
The elegant pancakes that she loved to make,
All the noses in town would quiver and sniff
In order to get just a hint of a whiff
Of the delicate, fragrant, most wonderful smell
That told them her pancakes were going quite well.

Her pancakes were feathery, fluffy, and flavory,
Tender and toothsome, incredibly savory—
Served with a syrup so pure and delightful,
That some people swooned when they'd bitten
     a biteful.

Now this excellent wife,
    with those pancakes delightful,
Had only one fault;
    but that one fault was frightful:
She would serve all the pancakes;
    when that was complete,
She'd announce very firmly,
    "There's no more to eat.
Just one to a person, and not
    any more!"
Though they'd weep and they'd
    wail, though they'd rage and
    they'd roar,
Though they fainted in hunger
    or teased her in fun,
She would always announce,
    "Every person gets one."
Though they praised her
    and said that her pancakes were flavory,
Tender and toothsome, incredibly savory—
She just waited grimly until they were through;
And then she'd say flatly, "No one gets two!"

She would plant her feet firmly and
   look very gruff,
Declaring quite firmly,
   "One pancake's enough."
And everyone thought
   how delighted he'd be
If he could have two cakes,
         perhaps even three!

Now one day a beggar came
    wandering down
The road that led right through the
    middle of town.
He asked for some food,
    and he asked for some gold,
And he asked for a cloak
    so he wouldn't be cold.
And he said,
    "I'm so hungry—it would be a treat
If someone would give me
    some pancakes to eat.
Why, I'd be the happiest fellow alive.
I bet I'd eat fifty—or seventy-five."

The townspeople giggled.
    What a chance for some fun—
To expect all those pancakes
    and get only one!
So they said, "My dear fellow,
    until you have tasted
Our Good Wife's good pancakes,
    your life has been wasted."

They smiled,
then they chuckled,
then doubled
with laughter.

Then they sent him ahead,

and they all
followed
after.

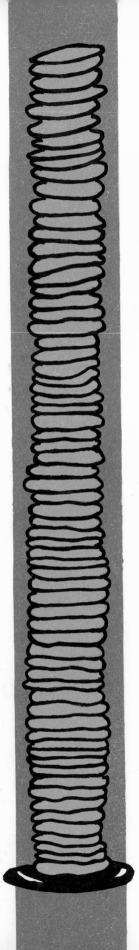

He went to her house and he knocked
 most politely.
"I'd appreciate pancakes,"
 he said very brightly.
"Of course," said the Good Wife,
 "come right in and eat it.
I'll just take a minute to measure
 and beat it."
So he settled himself and he
 loosened his belt
As he dreamt of how seventy
 pancakes could melt
In his mouth as he ate them.
 His fork was all ready.
His nose started twitching,
 his hand was unsteady.

"Seventy—eighty—or ninety! I'll bet
I could eat up a hundred—or all I
 can get."

The Good Wife came in then—his supper
  was done;
And there on the plate was a pancake—just one.

He gobbled it up;
    he consumed it with zest.
Then waited expectantly
    for all the rest.

The rest?
What a laugh!
The rest?
She was through.
"You've finished
    your pancake—
    now be off
    with you."

"Why, my Lady," he said, "that cake was so flavory,
Tender and toothsome, incredibly savory—
Served with a syrup so pure and delightful,
That I almost swooned when I'd bitten a biteful."

ST. JEROME'S SCHOOL LIBRARY
El Cerrito, California

"My Lady," he said then,
"be kind, I implore.
You're a generous
woman. Please, may
I have more?"

"I know," she said smugly,
"when put to the test,
Of all the world's pancakes,
my pancakes are best.

But let's not be greedy;
I've said this before:
I give everyone one;
but no one gets more."

The beggar looked up then and saw all the folk
Who had gathered to witness this practical joke.
"Aha!" thought the beggar, "so that is your
     game.
Well, I'll turn the tables and put you to shame."

"By the way," he said slowly, as if
     deep in thought,
"I oughtn't to say this, but maybe I ought.
She thinks that her pancake's the best
     of its kind?
                    It was good, I'll admit,
                    but I've so often dined
                         On pancakes so perfect,
                         so golden so tender,
               They put this to shame—
                    but I mustn't offend her!
               That pancake was burned;
                    she should not be so proud."

          Though he talked to himself,
               all this talk was quite loud.

She was shocked!

"It was burned? Then I'll bring you
     another,
And you'll see that it's better, by far,
     than the other.
I'll make just one more; it won't take me long
To prove to you, sir, that your statement
     is wrong."

He smiled to himself when she hastened right
　　back.
"Not bad," he said then, "but it seems
　　there's a lack . . .
In something significant it's somehow deficient.
Quite good, though," he said, "and you seem
　　quite proficient."

"Then I'll make you another.
I won't be gone long."

But each time she made one,
he found something wrong.

ST. JEROME'S SCHOOL LIBRARY
El Cerrito, California

Too little of this . . .
    too much of that . . .

Too highly seasoned . . .

now this one's flat.

However she made them,
  there was always a fault:
Too much butter . . . too little salt.

A little too soft . . .

or a little too tough . . .

Too much of something . . .

or not enough!

At last she exclaimed,
"Why, I don't understand,
For everyone says they're
the best in the land.
Everyone says they're
the best you can eat;
And no one else serves
such a wonderful treat."

And then she observed that her friends were
outside.
"Oh, prove that I'm right," the poor lady cried.
So everyone hastened to join in the fun;

And she mixed up a pancake to give to each
one.
It was all just as usual—one pancake apiece,
For the good woman hoped that this feast
would soon cease.

But all of the while she was busy with cooking,
All of the townsfolk kept looking and looking,
Kept seeing the beggar enjoying his treat—
All the good pancakes he ever could eat.

And he stared at them with a smile and a wink;
And that single wink made each one of them
   think:
If he could be satisfied, why couldn't they?
Perhaps they might get enough pancakes today!

They all ate their pancakes—the very last crumb;
But when they had finished, they all remained
dumb.
Then said the Good Wife, "Now, why don't
you praise me?
Your manners are dreadful—you really amaze me.

You know that my pancakes
are fluffy and flavory,
Tender and toothsome,
incredibly savory—
Served with a syrup
so pure and delightful,
That you've often
swooned when you've
bitten a biteful."

But
everyone
sat there,
and no one
would speak,
Until a child said,
in the tiniest
squeak,
"There's too much
butter . . . too little salt."

Then everyone joined in revealing some fault:

"It's a little too soft . . .

or a little too tough . . .

There's too much of something . . .

. . . or not enough.

They seem to be baked with a heavy hand.

They're far too spicy . . .
or far too bland."

ST. JEROME'S SCHOOL LIBRARY
El Cerrito, California

Although the poor lady grew tired and worn,
She continued to cook through the night,
    into morn.
Sniffing and sniffling she went without rest.
To prove to her friends
    that her pancakes were best.

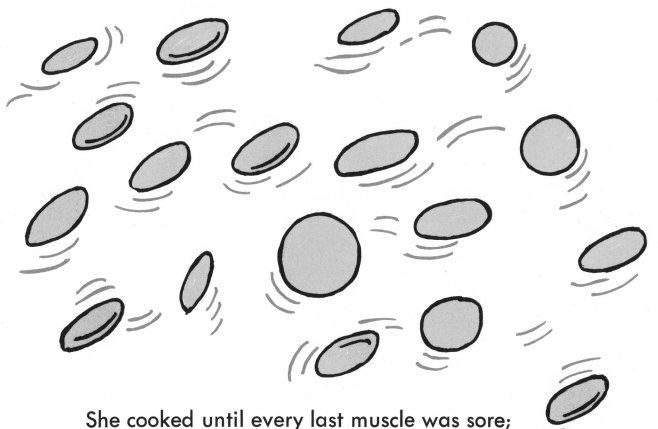

She cooked until every last muscle was sore;
And then she cooked more . . .
    and then more . . . and then more. . . .
She cooked them large pancakes,
    and then cooked them small;
And as fast as she cooked,
    they devoured them all.
And sometimes she thought that she'd never
    be through,
For each batch was wrong—
    and the next batch was, too.

But when she was ready to drop from exertion,
The people were filled, so they made this assertion:
"Although you've been cooking far into the night,
At last you've prepared a cake perfectly right.
Your pancakes are feathery, fluffy, and flavory,
Tender and toothsome, incredibly savory—
Served with a syrup so pure
and delightful,
That we nearly swooned
when we'd bitten a biteful."

Then she said, "Now that each has had
    one perfect cake,
I hereby announce that is all I shall make.
I hate to repeat this; I've said it before:
Each person gets one, and no person gets more!
One pancake to each, but that one must be
    grand.
And remember I'm still the best cook in the land."

"Excuse me," she said,
"now I must get some rest,
For I've never been through
such a difficult test.
But now that you've tasted and tested and eaten,
You'll agree, I am sure,
that I've never been beaten."
She slept then for days and for weeks it is said,
Before she could venture up out of her bed.
The townspeople grunted and puffed for I fear
They'd consumed enough pancakes
to last them a year.
They showered the beggar with silver and gold
And gave him a cloak so he wouldn't be cold.
For the lessons he'd taught them,
they rendered him thanks

And vowed that they'd often repeat these gay pranks.

The beggar said, "Some day I'm sure to return,
For wherever I go, I'll eternally yearn
For the pancakes so feathery, fluffy, and flavory,
Tender and toothsome, incredibly savory—
Served with a syrup so pure and delightful,
That some people swoon when
     they've bitten a biteful.

                              Farewell, alack!
                              But I'll be back."

ST. JEROME'S SCHOOL LIBRARY
El Cerrito, California